BEYOND THE SHELL
FINDING YOU BEYOND WHAT PROTECTS YOU

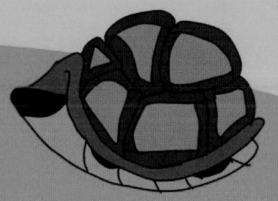

WRITTEN BY: WILLIAM BROWN

ILLUSTRATED BY: LISA SANTIAGO MCNEILL

EMPOWERMENT PUBLISHING & MULTI-MEDIA
CHILDREN'S BOOKS DIVISION

DEDICATION

To everyone that's has had any questions
about being their unique amazing self.

ISBN-13: 978-1090341716

WILL "THE TURTLE" IS EXPLORING

OUTSIDE HIS SHELL....

SAM "THE OWL" ASKS WILL
WHO HE IS.

IS IT THE COLOR OF YOUR SKIN OR
IS IT YOUR KIN?

IS IT HOW YOU WALK OR
IS IT THE WAY YOU TALK?

Is it what people say or
what they don't say?

IS IT THE PEOPLE YOU LOVE OR THE
PEOPLE YOU ARE SUPPOSED TO LOVE?

IS IT ALL THAT YOU KNOW OR
IS IT ALL THAT YOU WANT TO KNOW?

IS IT THE DREAMS THAT YOU HAVE OR THE DREAMS THAT OTHERS HAVE FOR YOU?

BECAUSE WHAT MAKES YOU YOU

Beyond the Shell is a series of light-hearted stories designed to engage the reader in an thoughtful look at life both from an introspective and retrospective stand point.

How often do we answer questions with what we have been told versus what we have discovered? When do we take a moment to 'ponder'?

About The Author

William "Bill" Brown shares his heart and thoughts through stories and adventures of Will the Turtle. He is a consummate story teller and long time Toastmaster.

William is an Executive Coach, Human Centered Technologist, Facilitation Leader and Professional Speaker. He is married to his lovely wife, Dalila, of 28 years and has four adult aged children Breanna, Jasmine, TJ and Aaron.

Connect with William on social media:
FaceBook: @TLCGuy
IG: @TheTLCGuy
Contact: 864-381-8139
email bill@shatteringthebox.com

About Sam

As my Drama Teacher at Langley High School in Pittsburgh,PA., Sam Rameas, imparted a large amount of encouragement and wisdom that took me much too long to appreciate and listen to.

Rest In Peace my wise friend.

Empowerment Authors Book Store

Empowerment Publishing & Multi-media produces children's books to inspire, uplift and empower our children to greatness. If you have a story that needs to be told that will inspire a child, let us help you to tell it. We offer coaching/publishing packages to suit the beginner and the vet! Our youngest author was only 7 year old! If she can do it, so can you!!

Empowerment Authors Book Store

We also publish stories of overcoming, and empowerment, self-help and personal development. Our unique model provides the author with writing support and structuring a business around their book so that they can make the most impact with their story. You lived through it, now use it to EMPOWER others!!

Contacts us at:
author@ePublishYou.com

Available Now!
Boom Hari
Empowerment Publishing & Multi-media

Available Now!
Dawn Petalino
Empowerment Publishing & Multi-media

Available Now!
Brian K. McNeil
Empowerment Publishing & Multi-media

Soon to be Released!
Subrina Sturgis Hough
Empowerment Publishing & Multi-media

Soon to be Released!
Tuyeni Akanke
Empowerment Publishing & Multi-media

Available Now!
Monique Alisa
Empowerment Publishing & Multi-media

Available Now!
Sammy O'Banion
Empowerment Publishing & Multi-media

Soon to be Released!
Martha Rushing
Empowerment Publishing & Multi-media

Available Now!
Belinda A. Houston
Empowerment Publishing & Multi-media

Available Now!
Shy Santiago
Empowerment Publishing & Multi-media

BEYOND THE SHELL
FINDING YOU BEYOND WHAT PROTECTS YOU

BEYOND THE SHELL IS A SERIES OF LIGHT-HEARTED STORIES DESIGNED TO ENGAGE THE READER IN AN THOUGHTFUL LOOK AT LIFE BOTH FROM AN INTROSPECTIVE AND RETROSPECTIVE STAND POINT.

HOW OFTEN DO WE ANSWER QUESTIONS WITH WHAT WE HAVE BEEN TOLD VERSUS WHAT WE HAVE DISCOVERED? WHEN DO WE TAKE A MOMENT TO 'PONDER'?

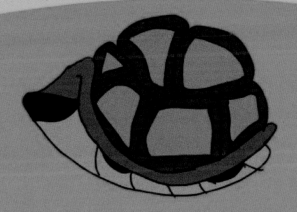

63099067R00015